Tales of the Dreamtime

selected from *Australian Legendary Tales*

collected by K. Langloh Parker

adapted by Vashti Farrer
illustrated by Walter Cunningham

ANGUS
& ROBERTSON
PUBLISHERS

How the Sun was made

Long, long ago in The Dreamtime, the earth was in darkness. Animals and birds lived by the light of the moon and stars and knew only the night.

During this time of darkness, Emu and Brolga had a quarrel. They screeched and squawked, feathers flying, beaks snapping as they chased each other up and down the banks of the Murrumbidgee. Finally in her rage, Brolga rushed to Emu's nest, seized one of the huge eggs and threw it with all her might into the sky, where it hit a pile of firewood and burst into flames. The yellow yolk spilt everywhere and flames lit up the earth below in a blaze of golden light that dazzled the animals and birds.

A spirit of the sky, seeing how bright and beautiful the earth could be, decided to make the fire every day. He and his fellow spirits collected a huge pile of wood and when they were ready to light it, they sent out the morning star to tell the creatures on earth.

But this wasn't enough because only the animals who were wide awake saw the star. So the spirits decided they needed a noise to announce the new sun and waken the sleepers. They thought and thought about who should make this noise, then one evening they heard the cackling laughter of Goo-goor-gaga the kookaburra, floating through the air.

"That's the right noise!" they said.

So they told Goo-goor-gaga that just as the morning star was beginning to fade he was to laugh as loudly as he could to wake everyone. If he didn't agree to do this they would never again light the magnificent sun-fire, and the earth would be in darkness forever.

So Goo-goor-gaga agreed to laugh just as dawn was breaking and he has been doing this ever since, making the air ring with his loud cackling, "Goor, goor gaga, goor goor gaga, goo goor gaga." This tells the birds and animals that dawn is breaking. Slowly the faintest pink begins to streak the grey of the dawn sky, for the fire of the new sun is gentle at first. By mid-morning the sky is filled with pale golden light for the wood has kindled. Then at noon, when the whole heap of wood is ablaze the heat of the sun-fire is at its fiercest. After that it gradually dies away leaving only the red embers of sunset. Quickly these too die out except for a few which the spirits cover up with clouds so as to light the fire the next day.

One must not imitate Goo-goor-gaga's laughter for if the kookaburra hears it he might refuse to laugh, and the spirits know that if a time ever comes when the Goo-goor-gagas cease their morning laughter, the earth would be plunged back into darkness forever.

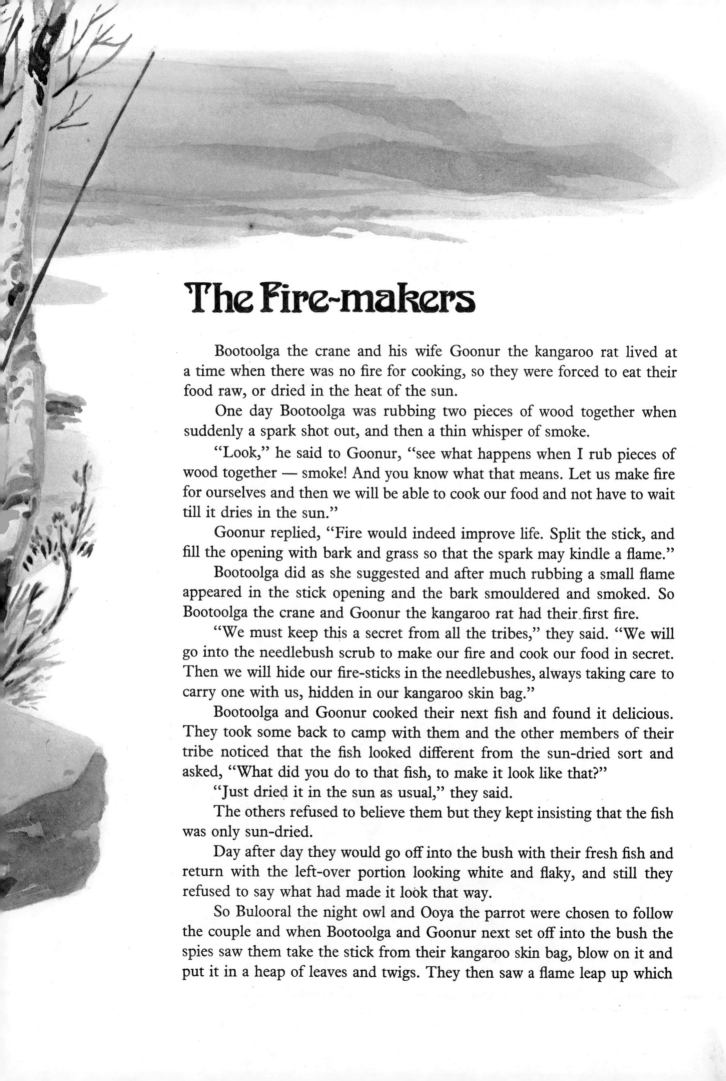

The Fire-makers

Bootoolga the crane and his wife Goonur the kangaroo rat lived at a time when there was no fire for cooking, so they were forced to eat their food raw, or dried in the heat of the sun.

One day Bootoolga was rubbing two pieces of wood together when suddenly a spark shot out, and then a thin whisper of smoke.

"Look," he said to Goonur, "see what happens when I rub pieces of wood together — smoke! And you know what that means. Let us make fire for ourselves and then we will be able to cook our food and not have to wait till it dries in the sun."

Goonur replied, "Fire would indeed improve life. Split the stick, and fill the opening with bark and grass so that the spark may kindle a flame."

Bootoolga did as she suggested and after much rubbing a small flame appeared in the stick opening and the bark smouldered and smoked. So Bootoolga the crane and Goonur the kangaroo rat had their first fire.

"We must keep this a secret from all the tribes," they said. "We will go into the needlebush scrub to make our fire and cook our food in secret. Then we will hide our fire-sticks in the needlebushes, always taking care to carry one with us, hidden in our kangaroo skin bag."

Bootoolga and Goonur cooked their next fish and found it delicious. They took some back to camp with them and the other members of their tribe noticed that the fish looked different from the sun-dried sort and asked, "What did you do to that fish, to make it look like that?"

"Just dried it in the sun as usual," they said.

The others refused to believe them but they kept insisting that the fish was only sun-dried.

Day after day they would go off into the bush with their fresh fish and return with the left-over portion looking white and flaky, and still they refused to say what had made it look that way.

So Bulooral the night owl and Ooya the parrot were chosen to follow the couple and when Bootoolga and Goonur next set off into the bush the spies saw them take the stick from their kangaroo skin bag, blow on it and put it in a heap of leaves and twigs. They then saw a flame leap up which the fire-makers fed with more sticks until the whole pile was ablaze. At last when the flame had died down they saw the couple take their fish and cook it in the ashes.

Bulooral and Ooya hurried back to camp to spread the news and when the people heard, they were envious and tried to think of a way to get hold of the fire-stick. Finally they decided to hold a corroboree that would be so spectacular that Bootoolga and Goonur would forget to guard their precious fire-stick, and Biaga the hawk could then steal it.

Once everything had been planned, they set about inviting the surrounding tribes and when the time came, the variety and colour of all the guests was fantastic.

Beela, the black cockatoo tribe, came with bright splashes of orange-red on their black skins, while the pelicans in contrast were almost pure white, only a touch of black skin showing where the white paint had rubbed off. The black divers came as they were, their black skins polished to shine like satin. Then came the Millias, the beautiful kangaroo rats from the pebbly ridges and after them the Bukkandi or native cat tribe, painted in dull colours but in all sorts of patterns. And there were grey and pink Galahs and green and crimson Billai parrots and bright little Gidgerigars, but perhaps the most dignified of all were the stately Brolgas. With their heads painted red against their grey bodies, they had been asked to give a display of their magnificent dancing.

When they arrived for the corroboree, Bootoolga warned Goonur that they must not take part because they had to guard their skin bag. So Goonur sat beside him and slung the bag over her arm, but she became so engrossed that the bag slipped from her arm. Just as Biaga the hawk was about to seize it, Bootoolga saw it and quickly put it back on her arm.

Biaga crouched back again while all eyes turned to the Brolgas who were just starting to dance. They came forward, bowed and retired, one, two, three, one, two, three, again and again, performing such crazy antics with such dignified expressions that the audience shook with laughter. In the excitement Bootoolga and Goonur forgot all about their kangaroo skin bag which slipped closer and closer within Biaga's reach. Suddenly he grabbed it, snatched the fire-stick from it and set fire to a heap of grass nearby, all before they realised what had happened.

When they discovered that their precious fire-stick was gone, it was too late. Bootoolga chased after Biaga but he was soon outpaced, and Biaga ran round and round setting fire to the grass as he went, until the whole of the performing tribes were surrounded by a ring of little fires.

And that is how the secret fire of Bootoolga the crane and Goonur the kangaroo rat came to be shared by everyone.

The Rain-maker Wirinun

There was once, long ago, a terrible drought. The rivers had all dried up except for the deepest parts. The grass lay sparse and brown and even the trees were dying. Bark humpies which provided shelter in wet weather lay rotting on the ground, it was so long since it had rained.

The young men grumbled among themselves, "Why aren't the rain-makers making rain? It's their job. But just look at everything; there's no grass worth speaking of, the kangaroos are dying, the emus and ducks and swans have all left. If we had any sense we'd leave too, for soon there won't be enough food for us."

Gradually these groans and mutterings reached the ears of the Wirinun or wise old man. He said nothing but disappeared for three days. He had gone to the big waterhole where he knelt down beside the water and placed in it a long painted stick decorated with white cockatoo feathers. Beside the stick he put two magic stones which he normally kept hidden in his belt or headband.

When three days had passed he said to the young men, "Now, take your stone axes, cut enough bark and make shelters for all the tribe."

The young men did as they were told and then the wise old man told every man, woman and child to follow him to the waterhole. When they were all assembled, he leapt into the water with the people jumping in after him. They splashed and played in the water for some time and then the

Wirinun came up behind each one and plucked out lumps of charcoal from each head of curly black hair, which he then threw into the water.

Then he stepped out and was shaking the water off when a young man grabbed him and threw him back. This happened again and again until the old Wirinun was shivering, and that was the signal for all the people to leave the water.

Then the Wirinun told all the young people to take shelter in a big bark shed and to sleep while he with two old men and two old women would stay outside. They loaded themselves with all their belongings as if they were about to set off on a journey and then walked impatiently around the shed.

Soon the heavy rain clouds began to mass overhead and the wise old man woke up the young people and told them to come out and look at the sky. Then he told them to gather all their belongings and hurry to their bark humpies. They had barely reached them when jagged flashes of lightning ripped open the sky and the thunder rolled and roared, smashing itself against the sky and terrifying the people in their little bark shelters. The children cried, the dogs howled, the women shrieked and the men went pale with fear.

Only the old Wirinun was unafraid. He went out in front of the shelters to stop the thunder and lightning from harming the camp and he began to chant:

"Gurri mooray, mooray,
    Durri mooray, mooray, mooray."

Soon there was a lull in the storm and a slight breeze stirred the trees

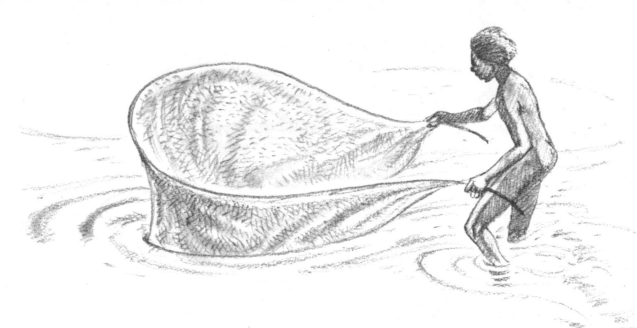

as a heavy silence settled over everything. Then the rain began to fall and it rained and rained for several days.

When the rain finally stopped, the country came to life again. The grass grew soft and green. Emus, ducks and swans built their nests once more and the kangaroos leapt in mobs over the plains. The people held a great corroboree to celebrate the skill of the old wise Wirinun but he took no notice of their praise. Determined to show how great his powers were he told all the people to go and camp around a large dry plain surrounded by tall dark trees.

Once the people were camped there the old man made the rain fall on the plain until it had formed a huge lake. Then he told the young men to take their nets and fish.

"What's the good of fishing?" they asked. "This lake was only filled yesterday. It's rain water, not river water. Fish cannot live in it."

But the old Wirinun said, "Do as I tell you and fish. If you catch nothing, then you can laugh at me."

So to please him, the young men cast their nets into the lake and when they drew them in they were heavily laden with all sorts of fish, enough in fact for all the tribes — and all their dogs!!

A Legend of the Flowers

After Baiame, the god of creation, had left the earth and gone to his
sacred Oobi Oobi mountain, the flowers he had left behind him withered
and died and nothing grew in their place. The earth was bare and desolate
and soon flowers became merely a legend which the old people passed on
to the young ones.

When the flowers went, so too did the bees. The women would take
out their bark dishes to fill with honey but they always returned with them
empty. There were bees still living and working on earth but only in three
sacred trees which Baiame had claimed as his own and the people did not
dare go near these.

The children cried because they wanted honey and the mothers were
upset because they could not give it to them, for the wise old men of the
tribes would not let them touch Baiame's sacred trees.

The spirit who saw everything told Baiame how the people longed for
honey and yet would not touch his trees, and Baiame was pleased. He
decided to give them a food as sweet as the honey which they loved. Soon
white sugary specks appeared on the gum leaves and sweet juice began
running down the tree trunks and hardening into lumps which the children
could gather.

The people were happy and their craving for sweet food was satisfied.
But the wise old men were far from satisfied. They longed to see the flowers
growing again and so determined were they, that without telling the people

of their tribes where they were going, they set out to find Baiame to ask him to make the earth beautiful with flowers once more.

They journeyed on for many days until at last they came to the foot of the sacred Oobi Oobi mountain, towering so far above them that its top was lost in the clouds. At first the sides seemed too steep to climb but eventually they found a foothold and then another and another until, looking up, they saw a ladder cut into the side of the mountain reaching as far

as they could see. Up they went, climbing one day, two days, three days until at last on the fourth day, they reached the top, completely exhausted.

They looked around them and saw a spring of water from which they drank eagerly and at once their weariness left them. Suddenly they heard the sound of a bull-roarer or spirit asking them why they had come. They told him how dreary the earth had looked since Baiame had left, how the flowers had all died and had not bloomed again, and although they had the sweet tree juice in place of honey, they longed for the flowers to make the earth bright once more.

Then the spirit ordered his attendants to lift the wise old men up into their sky-camp, which is a resting place in the sky where flowers neither fade nor die. Here they could gather as many as they could hold in their arms and the spirits would lift them back onto the top of the mountain so that they could return to earth.

Just as the spirit had said, the wise old men were lifted up through an opening in the sky and set down in a land of exquisite beauty with flowers

blooming everywhere, massed together in brilliant colours like hundreds of rainbows laid out on the grass. The old men were so overcome that they wept for joy. But they soon remembered why they were there and they gathered as many of the lovely blooms as their arms could hold. When they had finished, the spirits lifted them back onto the top of the sacred mountain.

Again they heard the spirit voice saying, "Tell your people that the earth shall never be without flowers again. Different winds will bring them in every season and the east wind will bring them in profusion and there will be blossoms on every tree and shrub."

The wise old men took the flowers that they had gathered and went down the stone ladder, across the plains and over the stony ridges to the camps of their people. The people flocked around them, overwhelmed at the flowers that filled the air with their beautiful perfume. When the old men had told them of the promise made by Baiame through his messenger they scattered the flowers far and wide, over the tree-tops, over the plains and ridges and wherever they fell, they have grown ever since. And the place where they were first scattered is called Girraween, the place of flowers. And thereafter trees and shrubs blossomed thickly again, and the earth was covered with cool grass and flowers as when Baiame, god of creation, walked on it.

Bohra the Kangaroo

Long ago there was a time when the night came down like a black cloud and veiled the world in darkness and neither the moon nor the stars could be seen. Bohra the kangaroo liked to feed at night but so that he could see he used his magic powers to roll up the darkness like a rug leaving it sitting on the edge of the world while the stars and moon shone through.

Bohra in those days walked on all four legs like a dog. One night while he was feeding he saw a cluster of fires ahead of him and he heard the sound of many voices singing. He was curious and crept closer to see what it was.

Closer and closer he came to the firelight and to the sound of the singing, until he saw a long line of strangely marked figures coming out of

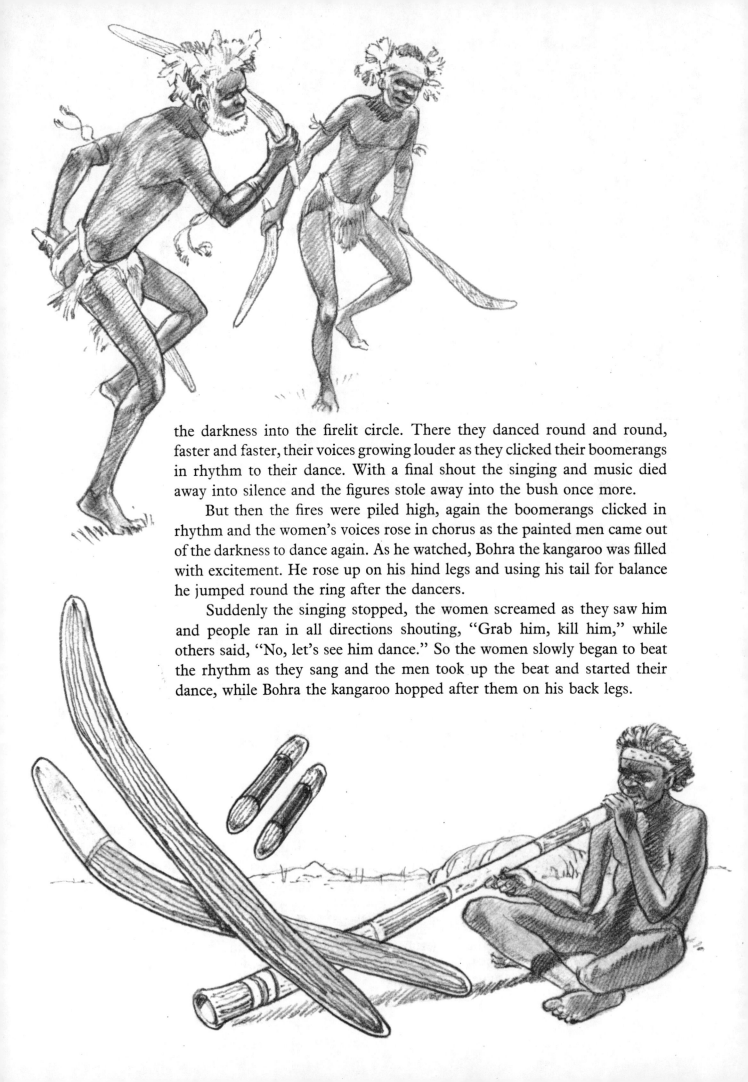

the darkness into the firelit circle. There they danced round and round, faster and faster, their voices growing louder as they clicked their boomerangs in rhythm to their dance. With a final shout the singing and music died away into silence and the figures stole away into the bush once more.

But then the fires were piled high, again the boomerangs clicked in rhythm and the women's voices rose in chorus as the painted men came out of the darkness to dance again. As he watched, Bohra the kangaroo was filled with excitement. He rose up on his hind legs and using his tail for balance he jumped round the ring after the dancers.

Suddenly the singing stopped, the women screamed as they saw him and people ran in all directions shouting, "Grab him, kill him," while others said, "No, let's see him dance." So the women slowly began to beat the rhythm as they sang and the men took up the beat and started their dance, while Bohra the kangaroo hopped after them on his back legs.

Far from being a terrifying sight, he looked so ridiculous that the singers and dancers burst out laughing. Then very stealthily the dancers crept from the ring, leaving Bohra on his own in the middle. After a while they returned, wearing tails of grass bound onto sticks. Round the ring they hopped, just like Bohra, their long tails waggling, and their hands held up like forepaws. The women could barely sing as they were laughing so much.

When at last the dancing stopped an old wise man said, "Well, Bohra the kangaroo came to our corroboree uninvited and for this he should be punished, but we won't kill him because he has given us a new dance. We must teach him a lesson though, so just as he performed tonight, hopping on his back legs, holding up his forepaws and using his tail for balance — so shall his kind move about this way from now on. Before he goes we will make him a member of our tribe so that he will keep quiet about the sacred rites he has seen tonight."

As a pledge of his keeping this secret they took out the canine teeth Bohra had. Ever since then, in sacred corroborees, the men of the Bohra tribe have worn false tails and danced the kangaroo dance, while Bohra and his kangaroo brothers have hopped about on their big back legs, just as he did in that long ago corroboree.

The Black Swans

When Wurrunna the aborigine returned to his tribe after one of his walkabouts he brought with him some weapons never before seen by the men. They came, he said, from a country called Wi-bulloo inhabited only by women and he had exchanged them for his possum skin rug. The women had promised to trade more weapons for more possum rugs. When the tribes heard this news they were so delighted they decided to go and barter.

So they set out with Wurrunna to the women's country, a plain beside the sacred Oobi Oobi mountain. Wurrunna had warned them of the dangers involved for he thought the women were spirits because they had told him there was no death in their country, nor was there any night as the sun never ceased to shine. Besides Wurrunna had noticed an evil smell on the plain like the smell of death, though the women had sworn that death never came there.

He suggested that they make a fire so that the smoke would destroy their scent before they stepped out of the darkness onto the plain and

Wurrunna himself would light a fire on the other side of the plain so that no evil would cling to them when they left.

Now Wurrunna, in his own way, was a clever man and he decided to take with him his two brothers disguised as water birds. As there were no birds on the lake they were sure to be noticed. As soon as the fire was smoking he would send his brothers swimming near the women's camp in the hope that when they saw the birds the women would forget all about the men who were to go onto the plain and the men would get the weapons they wanted.

Wurrunna told every man to take an animal with him and if the women interfered they were instructed to set the animals loose, so that in the resulting confusion the men could escape into the darkness once more. Every man found an animal. Some had possums, others had native cats, while others had flying squirrels or rats.

When they reached the place where the darkness was rolled up on the edge of the plain, they camped. Wurrunna and his brothers sped through

the scrub, skirting the plain till they reached the far side. There Wurrunna lit a fire, produced a magic crystal stone and turning to his brothers started to chant over them. There was an instant flash and they were changed into beautiful white swans.

Meanwhile the other men were smoking themselves with their fires. The women, seeing the smoke, armed themselves with spears and charged towards the plain. One of them, catching sight of the swans, cried out in surprise and the women's attention was drawn to the white birds on the lake, and they forgot all about the fires and the men rushed to the deserted camp for weapons.

But the women saw them and rushed back to their camp, not realising that the men still had one trick left, the animals. Suddenly dozens of little

creatures were released and swarmed all over the plain, possums, bandicoots
and many others, running everywhere, with the women hard on their heels.
While this commotion was going on the men dropped their possum rugs and
took as many weapons as they could carry and set off for Wurrunna's smoke
signal.

By the time the women saw them it was too late, for they had reached
the fires and smoked the evil of the plain from them forever and passed on
into the darkness. The women had no thought of following for they feared
fire as much as they feared the darkness, and though they turned to avenge
themselves on the two white swans, these too had gone.

The women were so furious they began to fight amongst themselves,
so violently that blood flowed freely, staining the whole of the western sky.

Ever since then, when there is a blood-red sunset the tribes say, "There are the women of Wi-bulloo fighting again."

The men returned to their own country with the weapons and Wur-runna travelled on alone towards Oobi Oobi, the sacred mountain, forgetting all about his swan brothers. They flew after him crying helplessly to attract his attention so that he might change them back into men. But Wurrunna was unaware of their plight and began his ascent of the stone steps on the side of the sacred mountain.

The swans soon grew tired of flying and came to rest on a small
lagoon at the foot of the mountain. The eaglehawks, who were the mes-
sengers of the spirits, were flying overhead and they saw the swans in their
lagoon. In a rage they swooped down and drove their huge claws and sharp
beaks into the swans' flesh. They clutched them in their claws and flew
with them far away from the sacred mountain, over the plains and mountain
ranges, away to the south. Every now and then they savagely plucked out a

handful of feathers which fluttered, still dripping with blood, down the sides of the mountains.

On and on flew the eaglehawks until they came to a large lagoon near the big salt sea. They dropped the swans onto the rocks at one end of the lagoon and began to pluck out their last remaining feathers when they remembered that they had not delivered their message and flew off to their own country leaving the swans on the rocks.

The poor swan brothers crouched together shivering, bleeding, feeling they were doomed to die far away from the rest of their tribe. Suddenly a shower of feathers began to fall gently on their shivering bodies and as they looked up they saw hundreds of mountain crows. "The eaglehawks are our

enemies," said the crows. "We saw them leave you to die and so we've sent you some of our feathers on the breeze, to warm you and help you fly back to your friends."

The black feathers covered the swans completely except for the few remaining white feathers on their wings. The down under the feathers was white and the red blood on their beaks remained forever. The white feathers the eaglehawks had plucked out took root where they had fallen and became flannel flowers.

The swans flew back over the camp of their tribe. Wurrunna recognised their cry but looking up he saw only black birds with red bills. Besides, Wurrunna had lost his magic powers for daring to climb up the sacred Oobi Oobi mountain, and sad as he was, he knew he would never be able to change his swan brothers back into men.